The Blackout

Story by Fiona Hardy

Illustrations by Jared MacPherson

The Blackout

Text: Fiona Hardy
Publishers: Tania Mazzeo and Eliza Webb
Series consultant: Amanda Sutera
Hands on Heads Consulting
Editor: Sarah Layton
Project editor: Annabel Smith
Designer: Jess Kelly
Project designer: Danielle Maccarone
Illustrations: Jared MacPherson
Production controller: Renee Tome

NovaStar

ISBN 978 0 17 033508 9

Cengage Learning Australia
Level 5, 80 Dorcas Street
Southbank VIC 3006 Australia
Phone: 1300 790 853
Email: aust.nelsonprimary@cengage.com

For learning solutions, visit **cengage.com.au**

Printed in China by 1010 Printing International Ltd
1 2 3 4 5 6 7 29 28 27 26 25

Nelson acknowledges the Traditional Owners and Custodians of the lands of all First Nations Peoples. We pay respect to Elders past and present, and extend that respect to all First Nations Peoples today.

Contents

Chapter 1

A Plan Goes Wrong

In a notebook in his school bag, Mason kept a list of all the things he was afraid of. It included heights, small spaces, bugs, planes, big dogs, storms, poison ivy, small dogs with big voices, and about sixty other things, too.

He wasn't really sure why he worried so much. He had an older sister who never worried about anything, even though their parents thought she probably should worry a bit more about homework.

Mason just found a lot of things scary. It was almost a talent, like being good at juggling, but a bit less useful. If he started a new sport, he worried he'd be terrible at it.

If he climbed the new rope jungle in the park, he worried he would fall off and break both arms *and* both legs. If he spoke up in class, he worried he might get an answer wrong.

It didn't really matter that his friends tried things and failed all the time. His best friend Oscar was terrible at tennis, but he liked playing it anyway because he had fun chasing any balls he hit over the fence. His other best friend Sophie had broken her arm on the monkey bars and had said having a cast was the coolest thing ever. It didn't even matter that he knew everybody else in class got answers wrong all the time, and nobody ever minded. Mason couldn't help it. He was just afraid. And more than anything, he was afraid of his own birthday party.

Mason's twelfth birthday was in two weeks' time, and he didn't think he'd ever dreaded something more. When his parents asked him what he wanted to do to celebrate, his first thought had been that he just wanted to have a great time somewhere that he knew he'd enjoy with Sophie and Oscar. Then he had remembered the one thing everybody in his class wanted to do this year: go to Up & Down.

Up & Down had opened three months ago on the other side of the city. Mason's family had driven right by it when they had to pick up his grandma from the airport, gazing through the windows at all the construction work finishing up. It was a giant, glass-walled building that had been painted like it was covered in moss. The ads they kept seeing everywhere – on bus stops and before movies in the cinema – called it the "best kids' climbing and caving experience in the southern hemisphere".

The whole place was filled with clip-and-climb walls. Kids could buckle themselves to a rope and climb all the way up to the ceiling. You could climb an enormous pretend tree or climb a wall that felt like a video game, with coloured bricks that lit up when you touched them.

There was one climb, called the Jokester, where every two minutes some of the blocky handholds would pull back into the wall and new ones would push out. If the climber was lucky, their holds weren't the ones that disappeared. But most of the time, people would fall off, laughing while they were held in place by the rope. But what everyone wanted to do most at Up & Down was to try the Dark Forest Caves.

The Dark Forest Caves was a tunnel system built to look like an underground cavern – a maze of escape rooms full of puzzles that you needed to solve to get to the end. Kids had to wear headlamps to see as they made their way through the small, dark passages, past dangling vines and swarms of flying bats. The ads made it look terrifying, so of course the tickets had sold out immediately.

Almost all the kids in his class had tried to get tickets, but nobody had been able to. Which is *exactly* why Mason asked to go there for his birthday. He knew that Sophie and Oscar had been desperately wanting to visit Up & Down for ages. Maybe if he said he did too, they wouldn't think he was as afraid of everything as he really was. Then, when his parents said no, they could just spend his birthday at the same trampoline place he went to last year. He, Sophie and Oscar could eat a whole pile of food and bounce around for a few hours until they got a stomach ache, then get enormous ice creams on the way home. And all the while, everyone would think he was actually really brave and that he had wanted to go to Up & Down.

It was the perfect plan.

"Up & Down?" Sophie exclaimed, spilling her bento box all over the concrete in excitement. "That would be so awesome! I want to climb *everything*."

It was lunchtime, and Mason had just told his friends where he'd asked to go.

"I can't wait to make everyone jealous," Oscar said. He grinned at Mason and said, "That's pretty brave of you, too."

Lily leaned over from the next bench and said, "You won't make anyone jealous." Lily's best talent was feeling jealous of everyone else, even though she was always doing fun stuff. "There's no chance you'll get into Up & Down," she continued, "and you definitely won't get into the Dark Forest Caves. They're booked out until Christmas."

Lily pointed at Mason with a carrot stick and said, "Also, no offence, Mason, but you don't even like the climbing wall over there in the playground. Remember when you climbed it one recess and couldn't get past the first handhold, then cried until Mrs Powell came and helped you down, even though you could have stood on the ground if you'd reached your foot out?"

"Lily, come on! That was six years ago," Oscar said.

Mason's cheeks were burning, but he forced a smile and said, "Yeah! I probably wouldn't cry until the second handhold now."

Everyone laughed, and Lily shook her head and said, "I'm just saying, it's more Sophie's and Oscar's thing than yours."

She wasn't wrong. Sophie was the bravest person in the class – the one who would have a go on the giant swing first at school camp or jump off the top of the monkey bars six weeks after breaking her arm the last time she tried it. Oscar would do almost anything to make people laugh, including being the first one to try the chocolate-covered crickets his dad had bought. One time, he'd stood on his head for all of recess to see how red his face would go.

Mason wasn't that kind of person at all. He was the one who waited with Sophie until the ambulance came when she broke her arm. He was the one who got in trouble for being late to class after he made Oscar sit up very slowly from his twenty-minute headstand so he didn't faint when he lifted his head back up.

"Up & Down is definitely my thing," Mason lied.

Lily narrowed her eyes at him, but it didn't matter. She was right – he wouldn't be able to go.

But when he got home from school that afternoon, his mum Mia was waiting with a suspiciously big smile on her face.

"I have some news," Mia said. "We tried to get tickets to Up & Down, but they were sold out."

"Oh no!" Mason said, trying his best to look convincingly sad. "Thanks for trying, though. I'm happy to just go–"

"But," she interrupted, beaming, "it turns out a friend from work knows the owner, and he pulled a few strings, and guess what? We got three tickets for you and your friends to go this weekend! And, best of all, we even got you a turn in the Dark Forest Caves!"

Mason's heart dropped. He felt sick. Why did he have to have the kind of mum who knew people who knew other people? In this moment, it seemed deeply unfair. He'd never seen her look so pleased. Even worse, he had caused this whole problem himself. He should have just kept his big mouth shut.

"Oh wow. That's so great," he said, trying to look happy.

"You can tell Sophie and Oscar tomorrow," Mia said. "You're going to have so much fun!"

"Yeah … fun," Mason said, and gave her a hug.

Later, when he went to bed, all Mason could think about were the bats, and the dark corners, and the vines falling in his face as he crawled along. He woke up in the middle of the night with a gasp and stared at the ceiling until he calmed down. Then, he wrote in his book of fears: *tunnels, caves, bats, vines.*

He could only get to sleep when he thought of Lily's face the next day at school and how she would look when she found out where he was going.

Chapter 2

Up & Down

It was Saturday morning, and Mason's mums were driving him, Sophie and Oscar across the city for Mason's Up & Down birthday. There was a wide, dark cloud hanging low in the sky over the tall buildings ahead, but inside the car, everyone's moods were as bright as summer.

"I want to go on the Time Climb first," Sophie said excitedly. "I heard if you beat the speed record to reach the button at the top, you get to come back for free."

"I'm going to climb the Jokester," Oscar said, wriggling in the car seat next to Mason. "It sounds hilarious."

"I want to have the High Climb Sundae," Mason said, trying to match their excitement. "It's the tallest ice cream anywhere in the state."

"I can't believe this is really happening," Sophie said. "Mia, you're the best for getting these tickets."

Mia turned back to them and smiled. "I'm just excited for all of you! Now, remember, your booking in the Dark Forest Caves is at midday, so you have to all be off the climbing walls by then. There are only limited spots, since while you're in the caves it's just your group. So if you're late, you don't get to go."

"I know they're called the Dark Forest Caves, but they can't be *that* dark, right?" Sophie asked.

"We'll be there!" Oscar said. "Even if I have to bungee jump from a different climb to the cave entrance."

"I don't think that's how it works," said Mason's other mum, Beck, with a frown.

Beck was the opposite of Oscar – she almost never made jokes, and she once said she was allergic to being silly. Still, she was a great mum, and she'd helped Mason just that morning when he was worrying.

"I don't even know what I'm afraid will happen," Mason had said. "I've read all the information about the harnesses and ropes they use. I know it's not dangerous."

"It's a new thing," Beck had told him. "Doing something new is always nerve wracking, and you know from the ads that it's going to be a little scary. Sometimes it's fun to be scared, but sometimes it's not." She'd given Mason a hug and said, "Just remember, you won't be alone."

Now, Beck turned up the radio in the car. She always had it on when she drove, playing ancient songs from twenty years ago, and she especially liked the weather report. The radio announcer's voice rang clear through the car.

"There are storms forecast for the west of the city today, along with gale force winds and an extremely high chance of rain. Sounds like a good day to stay inside, folks!"

"Aw, looks like we can't ditch Mason's birthday celebration to go to the beach after all," Oscar joked.

"It's a perfect day for an inside party," Mia said.

Storms were Mason's thirty-fifth fear. "Yeah," he said, looking up at the clouds. "Perfect."

Mason hadn't been sure what to expect when walking through the front door of Up & Down, but being hollered at by a giant bat was definitely *not* one of his ideas.

"HAVE A CLAMBER-IFFIC BIRTHDAY!" the bat shouted, waving its wings about. "MAY ALL YOUR HIGHEST DREAMS COME TRUE!"

"This is awesome," Sophie said as she stepped inside. Then she turned to the man-sized bat. "Can you fly? Can I ride on your back?"

"Do you have a spare costume?" Oscar asked, examining the suit. "It's just that I'd really like to wear it to basketball tomorrow. I think the wings will really help my game."

"I'm just here to say HAPPY BIRTHDAY!" the bat shouted, backing slightly away from Mason's friends.

"Thank you," Mason said politely.

"THIS WAY TO YOUR CLIMB-TASTIC INDUCTION LESSON!" the bat said, leading the way.

The bat left them with an instructor, who showed everyone how to use the harness system to go up all the climbing walls. There were a lot of straps, and two clips that were used to buckle into the rope on each climbing wall. When someone was buckled in correctly, a light on their belt would turn green, showing it was safe to climb.

Mason had brought his fear notebook with him today, just in case. He thought that later he might write "red light on the belt" in it.

"Okay, kids," Mia said. "You have an hour until your Dark Forest Caves session. Go have fun!"

Sophie grabbed Mason's arm. "Come on," she said. "Oscar and I will race you up the Time Climb. And sorry, but I won't go easy on you just because it's your birthday."

"Nah, it's okay," Mason said. "You guys go on ahead. I'm going to look around for a bit first."

"I'll walk with you," Oscar said.

Mason tried to keep his voice normal. "I'm fine," he said. "You go up and tell me what the different climbs are like."

"Only if you're sure ..." Sophie said.

"It's my birthday," Mason reminded them. "I make the rules. And my first rule is that you need to go have fun."

Oscar and Sophie shared a look. Then, with a small smile back at Mason, they ran to the climbing walls they'd been waiting to try, their belts jingling.

Up & Down was huge, with windows that stretched all the way up to the high ceiling. Mason could see right through them to the dark clouds that had gathered in the sky outside, and he watched the rain that was falling harder onto the glass.

Inside, it was nothing but laughter and colourful lights. There were so many high walls with climbs that Mason couldn't even count them all. There was one that looked like a giant green beanstalk with a pot of flashing gold sequins at the top. Neon lights flickered in the tiny windows of a skyscraper you could climb, making you look like Godzilla. Mason watched a little kid in another area jumping across the tops of poles that had been made to look like enormous mushrooms. When one of the jumps was too far, she fell, giggling, waiting as the rope automatically lowered her down.

He saw Sophie moving fast up the Time Climb, which was a thick rope hanging from the highest point of the ceiling. When she reached the top, she smashed her palm into a red button, and it let off a siren. An instructor walking around next to Mason looked up at the siren and applauded Sophie's climb.

Shortly after, Oscar appeared at Mason's side, breathless. "I've already fallen off the Jokester twice," he said with a massive smile. "I'm aiming for eight times."

"Don't you want to get to the top of the Jokester?" Mason asked Oscar.

"Getting to the top is nowhere near as fun as falling," Oscar said. "But I want to climb something with you. What are you going to do?"

Mason didn't know. It all looked colourful and exciting, and none of it looked fun. His heart had started to beat a little faster all the times he had watched a kid fall off, even though they'd been safe every time.

"I'm still deciding," he said. "I'll just watch you guys for now and let you know later."

As Oscar headed back to the walls, Mason looked over at his parents. They were happily sitting at a table eating a giant bowl of chips. Behind them, he could see rain streaking against the window. Thunder rumbled outside like rocks tumbling over each other in the sky.

Mia waved him over. "You haven't climbed anything yet," she said, as he arrived and took a fistful of chips. "Are you okay?"

"Are you thinking about your list?" Beck asked sympathetically.

"I'm fine," Mason said. He didn't want them to feel bad for him. He also knew that if his mums thought he wasn't having fun, they might get everyone to leave to go do something else. That would ruin Sophie and Oscar's day, as well as his own. "I'm just checking things out."

"We'll watch out for you," Beck said.

"Please don't," Mason said with a groan.

"Is it because we're not cool?" asked Mia, who had two chips hanging out of her mouth like walrus tusks.

Mason smiled at his mums and went back to the walls. He looked around again, took a deep breath, then went over to the little kids' section. The walls were lower, and the larger handholds were easier to grip on to. One of the climbs looked like a tree with little fairy lights strung through it. He waited underneath as a kid much younger than him made it to the top, pumped his fist in the air, then jumped off and let the rope lower him down slowly. On the ground, the little boy unclipped his belt and held out the strap to Mason. "It's so much fun!" he said.

Mason buckled in, waited for the green light to glow, then took hold of the first branch. *Easy*, he thought. He used his foot to give himself a boost onto the tree roots, then, reaching out for another branch, he tried pulling up with his other hand to lift himself off the ground.

Then he froze.

He wasn't touching the ground anymore.

Mason's heart started to pound in his chest. He gripped both the branches so tightly he thought his fingers might break through them. He knew he wasn't far off the ground, but he was too afraid to look down and see if he was wrong. In his mind, up seemed so far away, which must mean that down was also far away. He closed his eyes and rested his head against the cool plastic of the tree trunk, trying to calm down.

After a few minutes, he felt something pull at the leg of his pants, then a little voice called out and said, "Are you okay?"

Mason opened his eyes. It was the little boy who'd come down before.

"Did you get stuck to something?" he asked Mason.

If a little kid can reach me, Mason thought, *I can get down.*

Slowly, slowly, he lowered his left foot until it reached the ground. It didn't take long. It was like he'd forgotten that he'd only just started the climb. He put his other foot down and, burning with shame, passed the buckle back to the kid. He walked away from the climb, miserable.

He hoped his friends hadn't seen him.

He looked up to see Sophie running over to

him with a big smile.

"I was so fast on the Time Climb, I'm in the top twenty times!" Sophie said. "You should come and have a go! How many climbs have you done so far?"

"Just one," Mason lied. "There's too many to choose from."

"Want me to come with you?" she asked. "We can try one together."

Mason shook his head. "You go," he said. "I'll see you soon for the caves."

He watched her run back to the Time Climb. Oscar was hanging from the Jokester rope again and laughing. He saw Mason and waved. Mason waved back, smiling as hard as he could so Oscar couldn't tell how he felt inside.

Chapter 3

The Dark Forest Caves

Mason ducked into a quiet space near the bathrooms, just to clear his head. He could see the mouth of the caves on the other side of the centre, behind a crowd of kids trying to peek inside. The upbeat music and the happy crowd were almost making Mason think it wouldn't be so bad in the quiet of the caves, until another thunderclap rolled over the building with a heavy bang and he shuddered.

On the wall in front of him was a list of emergency numbers and a diagram of safe exits to use in case of an evacuation. He liked adding those sorts of things to his notebook – helpful information in case things went wrong (which had never actually happened) – so he wrote some of them down.

Underneath the diagram, he saw what looked like a map. It was full of lines and boxes and arrows. *It must be a map of their back offices, or maybe the laneways behind the building*, Mason thought. Pen in hand and trying to find any excuse to put off going back to the climbing walls, Mason decided to draw that, too.

The building rumbled again with the sound of thunder. The rain was even stronger now, pounding down on the high roof. As Mason watched, lightning lit up the car park outside, and the few people heading to or from their cars ran by the window with umbrellas. Even though it was the middle of the day, it was really dark.

Just then, there was an announcement over the speakers. "The 12 pm Dark Forest Caves session will begin in five minutes. Explorers, please make your way to the cave entrance."

Sophie and Oscar were by Mason's side in an instant. "It's happening!" Sophie said. "We're going exploring!"

"I'm going to be so scared," Oscar said, delighted.

The friends lined up outside the caves. Other kids were hovering nearby, looking at them with envy.

Mason tried to think about how lucky he was, being able to go inside when so many others really wanted to but couldn't. He looked up at the large double doors, which were made of broken wood and had signs all over them that said DANGER and DO NOT PASS and BAT COLONY INSIDE.

Mason couldn't write in his notebook with everyone looking, but as soon as he was done, he was going to list two new fears: *danger signs* and *the words "bat colony inside"*.

A man with a bat on his hat and the name "Dave" on his lanyard greeted them at the doors. He handed them some helmets with headlamps they could turn on if they needed, along with full-body plastic suits to pull on over their clothes. "It can get a bit messy," Dave said.

The suits were a bit damp and streaked with green. Mason put his notebook in the outer pocket, just in case he had to add something new while they were in there – like *claustrophobia*, once he'd checked how to spell it.

"Okay," Dave said, "once you enter the caves, you'll be the only ones in there. I'll be watching your progress on my screens, and I'll meet you at the other end."

He continued, “The aim is to get to the end in an hour, but not everybody does. You’ll know how long you have left, because the sun will “set” inside – meaning I turn the lights off! In the meantime, you’re free to explore as much as you want. There are places where you’ll need to climb up or climb down, there’ll be dead ends, secrets to look out for and some surprises.”

Sophie was suddenly looking a little less sure. “Wait, you turn the lights off?”

“She’s afraid of the dark,” Oscar told Dave.

“No, I’m not!” Sophie lied loudly.

“I can just make an announcement over the speakers that the sun has set instead, if you prefer,” Dave said easily. “We only turn the lights off for a moment, for effect. If you have any problems, there are emergency buttons throughout the caves that you can press. It might be a little spooky, but there’s nothing dangerous.”

Oscar bounced on his toes. “I am so excited I can barely breathe,” he said.

“Well, take a big breath,” Dave said. “Because it’s time! You’re going in.”

The wooden doors creaked open. Behind Mason, Sophie and Oscar, the kids who were fighting for a glance inside all said, “Ooooh”.

Thunder cracked overhead, and the building lit up from lightning at the same time. Wind howled outside, and the roof shook. Mason flinched, and Oscar reached out and gave him a reassuring pat on the arm.

"Good luck!" Dave said.

The lights flickered as the three friends walked inside. The wooden doors swung shut behind them, and Mason jumped.

They were in a dim, grey cavern, about the size of the bathroom in Mason's apartment, but the ceiling was way closer. Realistic green moss covered the walls, and the sound of dripping water played over the speakers. Mason was sure he could also hear the sound of wings beating from somewhere down the dark tunnels. Sophie shuddered and took a step closer to him.

A voice boomed over the speakers. "You are now in the Dark Forest Caves! The door has shut behind you, and the only way to get out now is to keep going. There are numerous paths ahead, but only one will lead you to the exit. Good luck, travellers." There was a pause. "You'll need it."

Mason squeezed his eyes shut for a moment, trying to remember that this wasn't real.

It's just a game, he told himself. *You can press the emergency button at any time.*

He looked around and saw one right near the door. He wondered if some kids came in here and immediately pressed it in a panic. Mason decided he wouldn't press it in this room, but he did spend a few satisfying moments imagining it.

Try one more room, he thought. *You can always press the next one, and then at least you tried. Your friends won't be mad.*

Sophie, the tallest of the three of them, nearly brushed the ceiling of the cave with the top of her ponytail. "They've done an awesome job making it feel real," she said, looking around in wonder.

Maybe too good, Mason thought.

"This is like an escape room I did with my cousin," Oscar said. "We didn't escape it, though."

"Are you still trapped there then?" Mason asked, trying to joke around. "Maybe it's just your ghost that's here with us."

"Definitely," Oscar said, then gave a long ghost-like wail: "Whoooooo!"

Oscar's voice echoed around the walls and came back to them. Even though Mason knew it was his friend's voice, he still flinched.

Sophie saw and said, "Are you okay, Mason? I know you were the one who wanted to do this for your birthday, but is it too much?"

"It's okay if we have to leave," Oscar said immediately. "It means we get the High Climb Sundaes sooner, right?"

Mason gulped. He could've just asked to do something more chill for his birthday, like pizzas and a movie. But no, he'd decided to pretend he was brave enough to be here, and now he actually had to be.

"I'm fine," he said.

"Okay," Oscar said. "So, which way should we go?"

There were two tunnels leading out of the room. One said THIS WAY and the other one said SHORT CUT.

"No short cut for me, I want to see everything," Sophie said, but her voice was less strong than usual. "Plus, it feels like a trick. Let's go the other way!"

The tunnel they chose was narrow. They would have to crawl through it.

Sophie went first, and Oscar smiled at Mason and said, "You go next. I'll be right behind you." Mason gave his friend a grateful smile.

Mason was glad his friends hadn't raced ahead. He crawled into the tight space. He could hear Sophie's breathing as they squeezed through, and the rocks felt damp under his hands as he reached in front of him.

"Check this out!" Sophie called.

Mason reached the end of the tunnel and stood up, then gasped. Oscar stumbled out behind him, then said, "Oh, wow!"

They were in another small room. The walls were covered in glowing crystals, shining a bright, luminous blue. Despite himself, Mason smiled. "It's really beautiful," he said.

Sophie reached out to touch one of the crystals, and suddenly they all turned red.

The room dimmed. Sophie gasped and stepped back, then reached out and touched it again. The crystals went back to blue.

Mason kept his eye on the one light that was still red – the emergency button. *It's there if you need it*, he thought.

"There's no way out of here." Sophie said, looking around. "I guess we have to go back."

"Wait," Mason said. "Look there."

On one of the walls there was a faint line like the edge of a hidden door.

Oscar went over and pushed the door. "It won't move," he said.

"I think we have to figure out how to open it," Sophie said. "Maybe I touched the wrong crystal before – I wonder if there's a right one."

"Great idea," Mason said.

Oscar pressed another crystal. Everything turned red again. There was another crack of thunder outside. Oscar pressed the crystal again, and everything went back to blue.

"Everyone, press all the crystals!" Sophie said.

Mason tried the one closest to him. It turned red under his hand, and he tapped it again straightaway.

The room lit up like fire engine lights, flashing blue and red as everyone tried all the different crystals. They'd almost run out of options when Sophie pressed the one right in the middle of a line Mason had pointed out, and everything turned green.

"Congratulations!" a voice boomed over the microphone. "You have completed your first challenge. Your path will now be clear."

The door in the wall opened, leading to another tunnel.

"Go on, Sophie," Oscar said. "You're our leader."

Sophie hesitated, looking into the dark space. The tunnels were only lit with tiny circular lights to show the path ahead.

"The emergency button's just there," Mason said. "Let me know if you want me to push it."

"No," she said, shaking her head. "I'm okay. Just ..." She tried to smile. "Just ... stay close, if that's okay?"

Mason had never seen Sophie like this. Once, when they were in prep, he'd watched her stand up to a bully from grade six who'd kicked over Oscar's chocolate milk. Sophie had stood between the bully and Oscar and screamed "That's not NICE!" so loudly that four different teachers heard and ran over. Sophie was the one who figured out how to ride her bike without training wheels before everybody else. And she had been there by Mason's side that time he got scared on the climbing wall at recess years ago – and every other time he'd got scared of something since. But she'd never asked *him* to stay close to *her*.

"Of course, Sophie," Mason said. He put his hand on her shoulder and smiled at her. "I'll be right here."

"I'll go first this time," Oscar volunteered.

As Mason followed Oscar, he looked behind at the emergency button on the wall one last time. *Maybe in the next room*, he thought.

When Mason stood up in the next cave, he almost smacked right into Oscar's back.

"Careful," Oscar said, pointing.

Right in front of Mason's eyeline was a stalactite hanging from the ceiling. And it wasn't just one, but rows and rows of them. Sophie came up behind him, and Mason grabbed her arm to stop her running head-first into them.

"Whoa," she said.

It was like being in an ancient cave. The stalactites hung low and were glowing a dull orange, dripping water from their ends. On the ground, there were tall stalagmites, pointed up.

"Creepy," Oscar said, his voice cracking. Mason realised then that Oscar hadn't told any jokes for about three minutes – a new record.

"Do we have to touch the glowing things again?" Sophie asked.

Mason touched one and nothing happened.

Oscar shrugged. "Is there another door?"

"Not that I can see," Mason said.

"There!" Sophie said. "There's a button to press on the other side of the room!"

She was right – there was a button hidden on the far wall, past all the stalagmites and stalactites.

Oscar started to head over, but then stopped and said, "I can't reach it from here – all these pointy things are in my way!"

"They're laid out like a maze," Mason said, looking around. "We can't squeeze through them – we have to follow the paths they make. Sophie, try going a different way."

She did, ducking under lower stalactites, but found herself stuck as well in the middle of the room. "I can't reach it from here either," she said, stretching her arm out towards the button.

Mason tried another way around the edge of the room, easing slowly around the stalagmites sticking up. Then, he was there – face to face with the button. He pressed it, and the top of the stalagmite next to him popped open.

"What's in there?" Sophie asked.

"There's a key," Mason said. A thrill ran up his spine. He'd been the one to find this for all of them. Maybe this wasn't so bad after all.

"What do you think it opens?" Oscar asked.

"Nothing that I can see," Sophie said, looking around. "It looks like this cave is a dead end."

Mason felt a strange sensation pass over him, like he'd already known this cave would be. "I think this path led us to the key, but it isn't the way to get out." He gulped when he realised what this meant.

"I think we have to go back the way we came," he said.

Chapter 4

Blackout

Mason, Sophie and Oscar were back at the start of the caves, facing the SHORT CUT tunnel again. Through the closed entrance door, Mason could hear the muffled murmur of people. The rain pounding the roof outside Up & Down sounded much closer, too.

"Let's go," Oscar said, pointing at the tunnel entrance. He ducked down and started crawling. Sophie hesitated, then bent down after him. Mason followed.

Mason didn't mind the rooms so much – he could stand up in them and remind himself the caves were just made up. Under the layers of grey and green paint, he could see things like power points and cords hiding behind poles.

But the tunnels they crawled through were narrow, and he had to be on his hands and knees.

When he was down that low, he couldn't see the power points or anything that brought him back to reality – only the floor in front of him. He felt like he was losing control in the closed spaces, like he didn't know where he was.

Mason's feet scrambled on the rocks. All the while, he could hear the faint sound of dripping water from the speakers. But mostly, he could just hear his own heart pounding heavily in his ears. He was going slowly, too slowly. He couldn't see his friends ahead of him. Thunder clapped outside, louder than it had so far. The tunnel shook underneath him. It was too much. Mason closed his eyes and put his hands over his head. He was alone.

"Mason?" a voice said softly.

He opened his eyes.

It was Sophie, her face glowing softly in the dim light. "You slowed down," she said. "I had to go ahead to find a space where I could turn myself around and crawl back to you. Are you okay?"

He shook his head.

"Just follow me," she said. "I'm going to crawl backwards, and you can crawl forwards. I'll be here with you the whole time."

Mason took a couple of long, deep breaths to try to calm himself. Sophie clasped his shoulder, "We'll get to Oscar, okay? And you can press the emergency button if you want."

"Maybe," he croaked.

Sophie shuffled backwards. "Come on," she said. "You've got this."

Mason reached forward and grabbed a rock. The moss on it was slippery, and his hand skidded out from under him, nearly making him face plant. He regained his balance, and Sophie said, "It's okay. You're okay."

He looked at the moss on his gloves. It had smeared green all over them. *Green paint*, he thought. *It's fake moss. Remember, it's not real. None of this is real.*

There was another thunderclap that made the tiny lights along the tunnel flicker. Sophie looked up at them and gulped. "You're doing great," she said in a small voice.

Mason looked at her properly. She was shaking. Sophie hated the darkness so much – she always had. But she'd gone back into it – on purpose – just to help her friend.

"Thanks for coming back for me," he said with feeling.

Suddenly, a flash of lightning lit up the tunnels, coming through the thin lines that Mason realised were the joins in the pipes they'd been crawling through. Sophie's eyes in front of him were bright in the flash. And then everything went black.

Sophie screamed. Her grip tightened on Mason's hands. They couldn't see anything! The tunnel was completely dark. The sound of dripping water that had been coming from the speakers had stopped altogether.

Oscar called out, "Guys! Can you hear me? What happened? Where are you?" He sounded far away.

"We're still coming through the tunnel," Mason shouted back. "I don't know what happened! Maybe it's part of the game? Remember Dave said something about the sun setting?"

"But it hasn't been an hour yet," Oscar called.

"No," Sophie whispered in front of Mason. "It must be the storm. It's a blackout ... I have nightmares like this."

This was like Mason's nightmares, too. He couldn't see where his knees were going, or his hands. But, somehow, it didn't seem as important as the fear in Sophie's voice. He needed to help her now and panic later.

When he got back home, he could write in his notebook that he was afraid of Sophie's scared voice.

"It's so dark," she said, her voice smaller than ever.

Dark, Mason thought. He reached up and switched on his headlamp. Light flooded the tunnel. Sophie had her eyes squeezed shut with her hands over her face. He reached up and switched her headlamp on, too.

"Sophie," he said, shaking her arm gently. "There's light now. It's okay, it's not dark."

She opened her eyes, squinting at him and blinking. "I forgot about these," she said, reaching up to touch her headlamp.

"Let's get to Oscar, okay?" Mason said.

Sophie nodded.

"Keep crawling backwards," he said, talking her through. "You've already gone through it to turn around, remember. You know it's safe. Let's just go slowly until we get to Oscar."

Sophie slowly inched her way backwards. "You're doing great," he said. "Just keep moving. Imagine you're a worm."

"Great, I've always wanted to be a worm," she said, almost smiling.

"Worms don't have to do homework, but they probably do have to wake up at 5 am to get eaten by the early bird," Mason said.

"I bet worms can't get Wi-Fi underground to play video games either," Sophie said.

While Sophie had been talking, she had moved faster, and Mason had crawled after her. Without realising it, she'd backed right up to the edge of the room Oscar was waiting in.

"Headlamps!" Oscar said, as soon as he saw them. "I can't believe I forgot!" He switched his on, and went on talking in a rush. "I'm so glad you're here. I was waiting in the dark! Alone! There was nobody to listen to my jokes," he added sadly.

The room was small. There were two more tunnel entrances leading out of it, and the walls of the room were dotted with little unlit light bulbs. Mason wondered what it looked like when it was lit up; right now, it looked sad and grey.

"Well, let's hit the emergency button and get Dave to get us out of here," Mason said. "It's too scary."

"He means for me," Sophie said.

"Well, there's good news and bad news," Oscar said.

"The good news is that there's a button right here next to me," Oscar said, pointing to a red circle on the wall.

"Great!" Mason said.

"And the bad news," Oscar said, "is that the button doesn't work."

Chapter 5

A Way Out

"What do you mean, the button doesn't work?" Sophie burst out. "It's for emergencies!"

"I tried it as soon as the lights went out. But you try," Oscar said.

The button was down near the bottom of the wall. Mason reached down and pressed it. It made a hollow click sound, but there was no light.

"You're right," he said.

"What do we do?" Sophie asked.

"Set up camp," Oscar said. "Light a fire. Watch the stars."

He was joking, but even his voice was wobbly. Mason said, "I think we should wait here. The button's broken, but they'll know where we are."

"No, they won't," Sophie said anxiously.

"Dave said he was watching us on a screen," Mason said. "So he'll know the last place we were."

"How did you remember that?" Oscar asked.

"I'm very good at listening to information about what to do when things go wrong," Mason said, and laughed.

"I'm too busy listening to the fun stuff," Sophie said sadly.

"I don't even know what listening is," said Oscar, and Sophie finally smiled.

"How long do we wait?" she asked. "What if it takes–"

Just then, the loudspeaker crackled back to life.

"Hi, folks," Dave said. "Bit of a problem. Unfortunately, the whole centre's lost power. It took me a while to be able to patch into this speaker system, but I'll be able to hear you now if you talk."

"The emergency button doesn't work!" Sophie said.

"I'm sorry about all this," Dave said. "You kids must be a bit shaken up. Have you got your headlamps on?"

"We do," Oscar called. "I remembered mine first."

Sophie and Mason rolled their eyes.

Dave went on. "Good job. We're working hard to get everything sorted out for you. For now, it's best if you sit tight."

Dave's voice paused for a moment, then continued talking. "We can't get in there just yet, but it's our highest priority. The emergency tunnel exits aren't working at the moment because of the power outage. The only working door is the one at the end – it doesn't need power, but it only opens from the inside, so I can't open it. In the meantime, you're safe."

"But trapped," Sophie said faintly.

Dave spoke calmly. "Just for a little bit. But you'll be out soon, okay? I'm going to call the power company right now to check when the electricity will come back on. I'll be right near the microphone the whole time. Over and out."

"It seems a bit mean to say 'out' when we are 100 per cent in," Oscar said.

There was another clap of thunder outside. "I hate this," Sophie said, sitting on the ground.

"Look at it this way," Oscar said. "Imagine how jealous everyone's going to be at school when we tell them that normal kids only get an hour in here, but we spent three days in here instead."

"You are not helping," Sophie said.

Mason looked around the room, and then stopped as his headlamp showed something on the wall opposite he hadn't spotted before. "Guys," he said. "Come look at this."

There was a small keyhole on the wall, glinting bronze in the light of their lamps.

"It's a lock!" Sophie said.

Mason pulled the key out of his pocket and put it in the lock. It turned easily, and a small door popped open beside it. There was a cavity behind the door with a piece of paper inside it.

Oscar reached in and pulled out the paper, then started laughing. "It's a voucher for a return trip to the Dark Forest Caves," he said.

Mason and Sophie groaned.

"Can we trade it for an exit from the Dark Forest Caves, first?" Sophie asked.

Oscar put the paper in his pocket anyway. "Maybe we can arm wrestle to see who gets it? Or to see who doesn't? That'll fill in the time while we wait."

"Or," Mason said, taking a deep breath, "we could get out ourselves."

His friends turned to look at him in shock.

"Mason's been replaced by a body double," Sophie said.

"There's no way our normal Mason would suggest this." Oscar said. "Crawling through tunnels in a blackout? Voluntarily?"

"And in the dark?" Sophie said. "I don't think so."

"I'm on Team Sophie," Oscar said. "I vote we wait. Besides, Dave told us to."

"It's because I'm scared that we need to go," Mason said. He looked around. "Our headlamps won't last forever, and two of us are freaking out a little," he added, gesturing to Sophie.

"Three," Oscar said, then added, "just to go along with the crowd, I mean."

"I'm scared of moving," Mason repeated. "But I'm more scared of our headlamps going flat in the middle of this room and being trapped in the dark than of trying to get to the end. I mean, we've been good at this so far, right? What if we make it? What if we get through fast and get out of here? I mean, if we're trapped in here, we can't even eat any lunch."

Sophie's stomach gurgled in response, and everyone laughed.

As their chuckles died down, Sophie sighed. She looked at Mason with an apologetic expression. "I don't think I can," Sophie said. "I'm sorry."

Mason walked up to her and looked her in the eye. "No problem. If you don't go, we don't go," he said. "Dave's right. We'll be safe here. If you're worried, then we'll stay."

"Okay," she said, letting out a shaky breath.

They all sat on the ground. Nobody knew what to say. Mason turned off his headlamp, just in case they needed it later. They waited in silence, listening to the rain outside and the sounds of the wind and the thunder still banging in the distance. Then, Sophie stood up.

"You know what," she said, "we should go. Yes, I'm terrified. But you know what? Mason didn't even want to come here at all, and we still made him do it."

Mason's mouth fell open. He thought his friends didn't know.

Oscar looked at his feet.

"I'm sorry, Mason," Sophie said. "I know you don't feel comfortable doing this stuff. At school the other day, when Lily said this wasn't your thing – she was right, and I knew she was. But we ignored that because we wanted to come here. Just then, you said 'if you don't go, we don't go,' but we didn't do the same for you."

"It's okay," Mason said.

"You still came," she said softly. "For us. You were brave. You crawled through tunnels because of us. You helped me because you know I hate the dark. And now, you're still trying to help, even though this is probably terrifying to you. Well, I'm scared. You're scared. Oscar - are you scared?"

"I'm pretending I'm not," Oscar said.

Sophie turned to Mason. "Let's get you out of this place and get you one of those giant sundaes you wanted before the ice cream melts in their freezer." She pointed at the tunnels out of the room. "We're going to escape."

Chapter 6

Bats!

There were two new tunnel entrances leading out of the room they'd ended up in. Mason turned his headlamp back on and looked up at the signs above them. One said CAVE OF BATS. The other said THE PIT.

"These seem like two terrible choices," Oscar said. "Maybe there's a sewer pipe underneath that's a more fun way to go?"

"Ew," Mason said. "I vote the Cave of Bats. Maybe because the power's out, they won't swoop us."

"I vote The Pit," Sophie said. "Because there's no bats in it."

"I vote The Pits as well," said Oscar. "I mean, The Pit. That's two votes. Sorry, Mason."

Sophie peered into the dark tunnel nervously.

"Sophie should go in the middle," Mason said. "Oscar, you go first. I'll take the back."

Oscar saluted, and headed in. Sophie nodded, took a deep breath, and followed. As they crawled along, Mason wondered if his parents were scared right now, too. They knew he was afraid of – well, everything. They probably thought he was crying in a corner right now. Mason was kind of surprised he wasn't crying in a corner, himself.

The tunnel started sloping upwards, using rocks (real ones, Mason was pretty sure) as places to put your feet and hands. Sophie almost slipped in the dark, and Mason caught her foot as she yelped.

"You're okay," he told her.

Oscar, in front of them both, gave a shout.

Sophie froze. "Are you okay?" she called out anxiously.

That's when they heard a much more familiar sound: Oscar laughing. "You have got to see this," he called out.

As Sophie reached the end of the tunnel where Oscar was waiting, Mason heard her say, with a smile in her voice, "This is the pit?"

Mason followed her out of the tunnel and sure enough, right in front of them was a pit. A ball pit.

There were grey and green balls everywhere, and Oscar was sprawled right in the middle of them, looking relaxed. “Come join me,” he said. “I’m having a ball.”

“You are so corny,” Sophie said, climbing in and immediately flailing. “Wait, it’s deeper than I thought!”

“There are probably still some kids from opening day trapped underneath here,” Oscar joked.

Mason looked around and spotted another door – this one shut, with a padlock on the handle. “I guess we need to find another key?”

“In the ball pit?” Oscar asked.

Sophie started digging in the pit like an excited puppy, sending balls flying behind her. “Search!”

“For what?”

“I don’t know! Writing on a ball? A picture of a key?”

“There must be hundreds in here,” Mason said, scooping with both hands. “How will we find one ball?”

They scrambled around for a while, until Oscar said, “Do you think this might be something?”

He held up a single black plastic ball and shook it. Something jingled inside.

“Open it!” Mason said.

Oscar popped it open and held up a key. “We’re geniuses!” he said.

They climbed up the side of the pit, and Oscar used the key in the lock. It clicked, and the door swung open in front of them.

Mason, Sophie and Oscar peered into the darkness of the new space as they stepped through the door. The roof felt lower than the other rooms they’d been in, and their headlamps were reflected in the glass of empty light bulbs.

“Can you see what the trick is in this room?” Oscar asked. “There has to be something.”

“There’s a tunnel over there,” Sophie said, pointing her headlamp off to the right. “It’s got a sign on the top. I think it says MORE TUNNELS THIS WAY, but it’s small. I can’t read it properly.” She stepped forward, and there was a creak and a click underneath her foot. Then, in eerie silence apart from a swoosh of air, a hundred bat wings flapped into their faces.

Oscar’s scream filled the room. Mason thrashed his hands in front of his face.

The bats were greasy and furry, and everywhere he moved there were more of them. They felt real, and they were all around them and they were ... not moving.

"Guys," Sophie called. "Stay still!"

Oscar's yelling slowly started to peter out. Mason stopped thrashing, closed his eyes, and took a breath. *If Sophie's calm, you're calm.* He opened his eyes.

There were definitely bats. Maybe not hundreds of them – tens, at most. And they were definitely, absolutely not real.

"I thought you said they wouldn't fly out at us!" Oscar said.

"I was just guessing," Mason said.

The bats were hanging from wires. They'd fallen on them from a net on the ceiling that Mason and his friends hadn't been able to see properly in the dark. They all had little unlit light-bulb eyes, and the ceiling had complicated metal tracks all around it. "I think they're supposed to have flashing eyes and swoop around on their own," Mason said, "and I bet they play loud bat sounds."

"I heard a loud sound," Oscar said. "It sounded like a bat scream to me."

"I think that might have been you," Sophie said.

"That doesn't sound right," Oscar said. "I'm always very calm."

"Now *that* is your best joke yet," Sophie said.

Mason touched the bats with his fingers. This had been one of the things he'd been dreading the most, but in reality, it was just a bunch of dangling puppets. Sure, it would have been scarier with the power on. *Or maybe*, he thought, *it might have been kind of ... fun.*

Mason looked at the ground around the door they'd stepped through. "I think there's an automatic mechanism that Sophie stood on. So even though the power's out, the bats were going to be released anyway."

"Huh," Sophie said, pushing on the loose part of the ground with her foot. "You're right."

"Where to now?" Oscar said.

"Now," Mason said, "we get out of here."

Chapter 7

The End of the List

Under the sign marked MORE TUNNELS THIS WAY, a row of green vines hung over the doorway. They were cut from a smooth plastic that was so cold to touch, it was almost slimy. Mason, shuddering at the feel of them under his fingers, held them aside for his friends so they could walk through.

In the next room, there were three more tunnel entrances. One said SHORTER CUT. The second said SHORTEST CUT. The last said MORE BATS.

"I have a question," Sophie said.

"Is it about bats?" Mason asked.

"Well, when we picked the last tunnel, we chose The Pit and not the Cave of Bats – but then we still got the bats! Why do you think that is?"

"Maybe we took a wrong turn?" Oscar said. "I wish we knew where we were."

Oscar and Sophie were looking at the three tunnel entrances, then glancing back the way they came, trying to figure it out. Mason furrowed his eyebrows, thinking about this room with its three exits. It looked like something he'd seen not that long ago.

He reached into the front pocket of his plastic suit and brought out his notebook, turning to the page he'd written on earlier. All those lines and squares and arrows he hadn't understood before suddenly became clear.

"Guys," he said, "I found a map before we came in. I think it's of this!"

His friends crowded around him. "Where did you get that?" Sophie asked, incredulously.

"I saw it on a wall, but I didn't know what it meant," he said. "But look, the way we just came – it's a trick. If you take the Cave of Bats tunnel, it leads through all these tunnels and then into this room through here." He moved through the vines, back into the bat room.

He pushed aside a thin curtain that was covering yet another tunnel entrance into the room. "See?"

"Sneaky," Sophie said, peering inside and shuddering.

"And if you go to The Pit, like we did, you end up next to the bat room, so you have to go in anyway."

"So, there's no avoiding the bats?" Oscar said sadly. "I didn't even know I was scared of them until they fell on my head."

"There's no avoiding the bats," Mason said. "But now I can find us the fastest way to get to the end out of these three tunnels."

His friends crowded around, and he showed them a square with lines coming out of it, just like the room they were in. "Look," he said, tracing a path with his finger, then pointing at the sign that said MORE BATS. "This way goes under the other tunnels and takes you back to the bat cave again."

"I vote we don't go that way," Oscar said.

"And the SHORTEST CUT takes you aaaall the way around the entire maze," Mason said, swooping his finger across the whole page.

"No wonder nobody finishes this in an hour," Sophie said.

"But the SHORTER CUT – here," Mason pointed, "I think it's telling the truth. It leads right to the exit."

"And there's nothing to scare us on the way?" Oscar asked.

"I don't know," Mason said truthfully.

The friends looked at each other. Sophie's headlamp flickered, and she grabbed onto Mason's arm. "I vote we take the chance," she said.

Mason pocketed his map, then stood in front of the tunnel that said SHORTER CUT. He dropped to his knees and started to crawl.

"Did you see that?" Mason heard Sophie whisper behind him. "He's going first!"

Mason hadn't even thought about it, but here he was: leading the way through a tunnel when he didn't even know what was at the end. It could be another room they'd be stuck in until the power returned. If it was, he'd have a lot of time to write down all of his new fears, at least.

The tunnel started to slope upwards so much that there were handholds drilled into the side to grab. It reached a high point, then sloped back down again. The floor was soft instead of rocky, and Mason almost considered going down it like a slide.

Maybe next time, he thought. He smiled at himself.

"You having fun?" he called back.

"Less talking, more moving!" Sophie said, and Mason grinned.

He was starting to feel like they were close to the end when a deep rumble sounded ahead of them. It didn't sound like thunder. Sophie must have heard it, too, because she called out.

"What was that? Is it a cave-in?"

"It's not a real cave, remember?" Oscar shouted from further behind. "But, uh, Mason, it's not a cave-in, is it?"

"It's thunder!" he called back, trying to sound like he believed it.

"I don't think so," Sophie said.

The sound struck again, even louder. Mason gulped, and suddenly, Sophie was right at his heels, barrelling into him. He lost his grip on the sloping floor, and then he and Sophie were sliding down the tunnel after all, Oscar right behind them, screaming all over again. The three of them slipped and slid in the painted moss all the way down, until they found themselves sprawled on the floor in a little dark room on what felt like fake grass.

Mason and Oscar heard Sophie gasp, and swung their headlamps towards her just as Oscar's headlamp flickered and went dead.

"Oscar," Mason said. "Your lamp. It's ..."

"Forget the lamp," Sophie said, pulling Mason over and pointing his head in the right direction.

There was a door across from them. Tall and wooden, just like the one at the start. In painted words across the wood, it said CONGRATULATIONS! YOU HAVE FINISHED THE DARK FOREST CAVES ADVENTURE! PUSH THE DOOR TO EXIT!

Underneath the words was a timer. It was blank.

"I reckon that took us five minutes. Six, max," Oscar said, tapping it with his knuckles.

"Stop joking around and open the door!" Sophie yelled, shoving them both towards it.

Together, they braced against the door and pushed.

"... So," Mason said, "It turned out it wasn't a cave-in at the end after all!"

He was telling the story all over again. It was nearly a week since the blackout that had shut down half of the city, and he'd lost track of the number of times he'd told it.

He'd had to tell the story to Lily and the rest of the class. Then, he'd had to tell all the other grade six classes, the kids at after-school care and the vice principal, who wanted to know what everyone else was talking about.

"If it wasn't a cave-in, what was it?" Mrs Powell asked.

"It was my mums," Mason said. "They heard our voices when we got closer, and they were banging on the door and shouting out to encourage us. But we couldn't hear them! We could just hear the noise of them thumping on the door."

"Wow," Mrs Powell said. "And to think I was scared when the power went out, and all I was doing was sitting at home watching the football on TV!"

A few other kids had started hovering nearby when he told the story, and when Mrs Powell smiled and left, they dispersed, too. Mason started to head back to his friends when the bell rang. He waited in line outside his class, where everyone had started talking about Lily's upcoming birthday again.

It was at the end of the month, and she couldn't decide what to do. First, it was going to be a swimming party, then a slime-making one, then just a comedy movie night. "But I've got a better plan now," Lily was saying. "I told my family about what happened at Mason's birthday, and they're going to set up a fake blackout game in our house and backyard, with tunnels and dark rooms and spooky bats and everything."

"The bats weren't that spooky," Oscar lied.

"Why don't you just go to Up & Down?" Sophie asked.

"But what if the blackout doesn't happen again?" Lily replied. "That's the whole point! Then we wouldn't get to be brave and solve puzzles and be a hero, like Mason was when he saved Sophie and Oscar."

"He sure did," Sophie said, nodding. "AND he let me have some of his sundae at the end, so he's a double hero."

Mason smiled to himself. Not about the sundae – though it did taste pretty good after everything – but about being called a hero.

He'd been called a lot of things in his life, but never a hero. He didn't really feel like one. But the more he thought about it, the more he realised he did feel different. Things didn't seem quite as scary now that he'd been trapped in the dark in a tunnel, and since he'd realised that everybody had something they were afraid of.

When the end-of-day bell rang, Mason, Sophie and Oscar left class and turned to walk to the back gate, like they always did together. But this time, Mason stopped and said, "I've just got to do something, okay? You guys go home without me. I'll see you tomorrow."

Sophie and Oscar waved and headed off. Mason waited until they were out of sight, then went to the playground.

The wind rustled the leaves in the trees nearby as he walked past the monkey bars and the swinging bridge. A grade four kid was standing at the top of the slide, reaching her hands down for her little sister, encouraging her to run up it and into her arms. The little sister was shaking her head and trying not to cry.

Mason caught the little sister's eye and smiled at her. "It's okay to be scared," he said to her.

"It's too high," she wailed.

"Maybe one day it won't be," he told her. "And you're just going to get bigger and stronger."

She sniffed. "Like a superhero?"

"Exactly," Mason said.

He gave her a thumbs up and walked around

the other side of the slide.

The climbing wall was still there. It had always seemed huge – especially when he was in prep, when he'd become stuck only centimetres off the ground. Today, it didn't really seem so tall. If he raised his hands up, he'd be most of the way up already.

He didn't know how climbing it would end: if he'd fall in the tanbark and get it all over his back – or if he'd make it all the way up. Somehow, it didn't matter so much.

He got out his fear notebook and found number three – *climbing walls* – and crossed it out.

He reached out, took a breath, and started to climb.